Ben & Holly's Little Kingdom™

The Little Forest

Elf Oak Wood

Gaston's Cave

Elf Windmill

Great Elf Tree

Elf Farm

Little Castle

The Meadow

Mrs Witch's House

Royal Golf Course

Frog Pond

N
W · E
S

The Bramble Woods

King Thistle's New Clothes

Today's adventure starts at the Little Castle . . .

King and Queen Marigold
are coming to the Little
Castle today, but Queen
Thistle is worried.
"They are very fashionable,"
she warns the King.
"I don't want them to think
we look scruffy!"

King Thistle looks very scruffy. His clothes are covered in splodges and cake crumbs! "That is why I have ordered the Elf Taylor to make you some new clothes," says the Queen.

While King Thistle has a bath, the Elf Taylor arrives with the new clothes.

"Oooh! Very nice!" says Nanny Plum.

"Oh, please, don't prod it!" cries the Elf Taylor. "This is a very delicate fabric, which means you must not clean it with magic," he warns them as he leaves.

Queen Thistle thinks she can see a speck of dirt on the new clothes. She brushes it with a feather duster, but it leaves a big dirty mark!

6

"Mummy!" cries Princess Holly. "You've made Daddy's new clothes dirty!"
Nanny Plum has an idea. "There's nothing clothes like better than a good hot soapy wash!" she says, merrily.

Nanny Plum puts the new clothes in the washing machine.
Holly goes to collect the King's old scruffy clothes, too.
"We're going to wash all your clothes!" she tells King Thistle.
"OK!" says the King, singing happily from the bath.

Holly, Ben and Nanny wait by the washing machine, until they hear **DING!**
"Finished!" sings Holly.
But when Nanny takes out the clothes, they've all shrunk! Oh, dear.
"Maybe, when the clothes are dry, they'll go back to their normal size?" suggests Ben.

"Yes Ben! I'll just do a simple spell to dry them!" says Nanny. She waves her magic wand.
Abracadabra Make Clothes Dry.
Thunder and Lightning, Flame and Fire!

Oh no! The Elf Taylor said not to use magic – and now the clothes are burnt! But Holly has one more idea . . .

13

"We can make magic clothes!" cries Holly.
First, Nanny Plum needs something
shoe-shaped to turn into shoes.
"Carrots!" says Ben.

14

Nanny waves her magic wand and **POP!**
The carrots turn into special new shoes.
Then, she makes a jacket from a tomato
and a crown from a lemon!

While King Thistle gets changed, Ben, Nanny Plum and Princess Holly go to meet King and Queen Marigold. "King Thistle won't be a moment, he's just changing into his new clothes," says Nanny Plum.

"New clothes!" says King Marigold, excitedly. "That sounds interesting!"

17

Soon, King Thistle appears.

"Oh, ho, ho! That's fantastic!" gasps King Marigold.

"So fresh and exciting! Ah, ha, ha!" marvels Queen Marigold.

They love the King's outfit! What a relief.

But then, the clothes start making a strange sound . . .

POP! POP! King Thistle's shoes have turned back into carrots!
PARP! The jacket is a tomato again!
TOOT! The crown changes into a lemon!
"Ooh, I say!" gasp King and Queen Marigold.

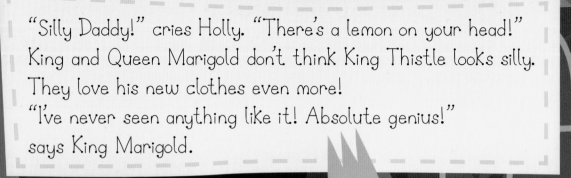

"Silly Daddy!" cries Holly. "There's a lemon on your head!"
King and Queen Marigold don't think King Thistle looks silly.
They love his new clothes even more!
"I've never seen anything like it! Absolute genius!"
says King Marigold.

King Thistle just looks a bit confused.
Then his tummy rumbles. It's time for dinner!
"I can make anything you like," says Nanny.
"As long as you don't want carrots, tomatoes
or lemons!"

Goodbye for now!